SELINA AND THE SHOO-FLY PIE

Written by BARBARA SMUCKER
Illustrated by JANET WILSON
Quilts by Lucy Anne Holliday

Stoddart
Kids
TORONTO • NEW YORK

The author and illustrator would like to acknowledge helpful information from:
The Early History of Jakobstettel by Virgil Emerson Martin; Susan Burke and the staff of the Joseph
Schneider Haus in Kitchener, Ontario; Milo Shantz, civic, business, and church leader in St. Jacobs, Ontario;
Laura Bergey; and Shoo Fly pie bakers in Bluffton, Ohio, who shared their recipes and pies.

Text copyright © 1998 by Barbara Smucker
Illustrations copyright © 1998 by Janet Wilson
Photography by Ian Crysler

We acknowledge the Canada Council for the Arts and the
Ontario Arts Council for their support of our publishing program.

Published in Canada in 1998 by
Stoddart Kids,
a division of Stoddart Publishing Co. Limited
34 Lesmill Road
Toronto, Canada M3B 2T6
Tel (416) 445-3333 Fax (416) 445-5967
E-mail Customer.Service@ccmailgw.genpub.com

Published in the United States in 1999 by
Stoddart Kids,
a division of Stoddart Publishing Co. Limited
180 Varick Street, 9th Floor
New York, New York 14207
Toll free 1-800-805-1083
E-mail gdsinc@genpub.com

Distributed in Canada by
General Distribution Services
30 Lesmill Road
Toronto, Canada M3B 2T6
Tel (416) 445-3333 Fax (416) 445-5967
E-mail Customer.Service@ccmailgw.genpub.com

Distributed in the United States by
General Distribution Services
85 River Rock Drive, Suite 202
Buffalo, New York 14207
Toll free 1-800-805-1083
E-mail gdsinc@genpub.com

Canadian Cataloguing in Publication Data

Smucker, Barbara, 1915–
Selina and the shoo-fly pie

ISBN 0-7737-3018-4

I. Wilson, Janet, 1952–   .   II. Title.

PS8537.M82S44   1998   jC813'.54   C96-932256-9
PZ7.S68Se   1998

Printed and bound in Hong Kong, China by
Book Art Inc., Toronto

To Edna Staebler,
a friend and renowned author of cookbooks,
especially Food that Really Schmecks,
and the best cook of Pennsylvania Dutch food
in Waterloo County, Ontario.
— B.S.

For Grace's girls, Kath, Jude and Emma,
for their friendship.
— J.W.

Selina stood happily before the open window of her own
little bedroom in their new family home. It had been
built with freshly cut boards from the sawmill where
Father worked. In just one year since they had all
moved from Pennsylvania to Upper Canada, Selina had grown a
whole inch.

Selina's new bed stood beside her, covered with Grandmother's brightly patterned Bear Paw quilt. She rubbed her hands gently over the dark green patches from Grandmother's wedding dress.

Selina took a deep breath. The breeze drifting through the window smelled of freshly plowed fields. Behind them, white trilliums were peeping around willow trees that lined the shores of the Conestoga River. A robin was busily building a nest in the maple tree close by.

"I love our new house and our new village of St. Jacobs," Selina wanted to shout, but whispered instead. She touched the Bear Paw quilt one more time. The only thing that could make the day more perfect would be . . .

"Selina!" Mother called from the kitchen. "I need your help."

Selina ran down the stairs and almost fell over her little brother Benjamin, who held out his arms to greet her.

"Selina." Mother shook her head. "Be more careful. You are growing up. Already you are seven and this fall you will start grade two."

"School!" Selina cried, hugging Benjamin and carrying him to the front window. "Look down the road, Benji. Where it turns you can see the corner of my little log schoolhouse."

Mother smiled, handing Selina an apron and cap. "There is more to do." She reached for Benjamin and placed him in his high chair.

Selina was very excited. Uncle Isaac, Aunt Minerva, and Selina's four cousins were coming from Waterloo for dinner. She and Mother had worked most of the day until the kitchen was full of delicious smells. Now, they set the long table with extra places for their company.

Selina stopped suddenly to listen. She could hear the clap-clapping of horses' hooves coming down their lane. She lifted Benjamin from his high chair and ran with him to the front porch. From the sawmill Father must have seen the visitors coming too, for he was striding behind the buggy as it slowed to a stop and everyone clambered down.

"Our house is almost like yours, Clara," Selina burst out, holding her eldest cousin's hands. "Come inside, I'll show you."

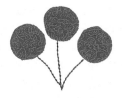

Coats and hats were hung on a peg rail along the kitchen wall and everyone found a place at the table. They bowed their heads for silent prayer.

Scalloped potatoes, ham, chopped pepper cabbage, bean salad with sour cream dressing, fresh bread, three kinds of jam, and cut green beans were passed down the table until every plate was full.

"It was so good I cannot eat another bite," Uncle Isaac said, as he cleaned his plate.

"Ach," Father laughed. "There is pie yet. Without pie at the end of a meal, I wouldn't feel I was finished."

Selina carried two Dutch apple pies directly from the oven. Everyone helped themselves to a slice.

When they were about to leave the table, Uncle Isaac made a surprise announcement.

"I have a letter to read from someone very special in Pennsylvania," he teased.

"Grandmother!" Selina gasped.

Uncle Isaac slowly opened the letter and began to read:

My Dear Ones,

What a hard time it is for everyone, especially our people, in this country divided by war. We Mennonites are against slavery and we want this land to be united, yet we cannot take sides and be part of the terrible fighting. For this we are resented and sometimes even hated.

Last week our Jacob and his family had to flee to us from Virginia. Their farm, the house, the barn and all the outbuildings were burned to the ground. Many of their neighbors were killed, but their family escaped across the border and will live with us.

It is their son, Henry, who suffers the most. He cannot eat or sleep. We think it would be good for him to visit you in Upper Canada. I have booked passage for Henry and me on the train that comes to Waterloo next week. We will spend the month of May with you. Selina and I will bake bread and Henry's favorite, Shoo-Fly Pie.

"Isaac!" Selina's father cried. "That means the train will arrive in two days!"

Selina's mind raced as the company left that night. The first thing she would do was show Grandmother her newly finished quilt and the little corner she had stitched all by herself.

For two whole days she thought about Grandmother's letter while images of the terrible war sent chills through her body. And for two whole days she wondered about those funny-sounding pies. Poor Henry. If he liked Shoo-Fly Pies, she would help bake them, whatever they were.

Mother and Selina scurried about the cellar, checking the shelves where loaves of homemade bread and pies were stored. There were canned fruits, vegetables and crocks of apple butter. Upstairs, the pantry was well stocked with sugar, molasses, pickles and butter. Finally they both agreed there was plenty for everyone.

"This will be Grandma and Henry's home away from home," Selina sang, as she grabbed an old straw hat and slipped out the back door to gather every fresh egg she could find in the chicken house.

A sparkling spring day dawned for the arrival of the
Pennsylvania visitors. Butterflies fluttered around the porch as
Selina and Benjamin waited on tiptoes to catch the first glimpse of
Uncle Isaac's buggy. They were beginning to think it would never
come when at last it appeared at the bend in the road.

"They're here!" Selina shouted as she ran out to meet them.

An instant later Selina was in Grandmother's arms.

Then Selina noticed a tall, thin boy. His brown hair blew in rippling curls, but his dark eyes were filled with fear. Henry. Selina reached out and took his limp hand.

Father joined them. "Welcome, Henry," he smiled and placed his strong arm around Henry's shoulders. "I have something I want to show you later, after you have had a rest. New logs have just come to the sawmill and they must be cut into boards. You might be interested in watching."

Henry barely looked up, but Selina thought she noticed a slight expression of interest on his face.

"I don't need to rest," he said, his voice just above a whisper. Selina squeezed his hand and smiled at him.

"Good! Then we will go right now." Without hesitating, Father took Henry's other hand and started walking him down the road towards the sawmill. "We'll be back in time for dinner," he called over his shoulder.

"Bless your father," Grandmother said, as she wiped her eyes and entered the new frame house.

Selina immediately took Grandmother upstairs to see her treasured Bear Paw quilt.

"I think of you every night, Grandma," Selina said. "But it's nicer to have you here."

Grandmother smiled. "Still, this will keep you warm next winter when I'm back in Pennsylvania. I'm happy that you have it, Selina. And just look at your stitches! Some day you will be a quilter, too."

After Grandmother saw her room and Benjamin had been put to sleep in his bed, Grandmother and Selina went to the kitchen to begin baking.

Selina was about to ask about the funny-sounding pies when Grandmother whispered, "I have something new and delicious to teach you to bake. It's called Shoo-Fly Pie and it's Henry's favorite." Grandmother collected everything she needed from the pantry, especially molasses. She laughed as she looked up where flies were already buzzing, as if they were waiting for something.

All afternoon the two worked steadily making pie crusts, filling them with molasses and sprinkling the tops with crumbs. Finally, pie after pie was set on the kitchen table to cool.

"Ach, Selina!" Grandmother cried. "The flies are swarming!"

"Shoo-Fly Pie!" Selina laughed. "Now I know where the name came from. I think the flies must like these pies as much as Henry does!"

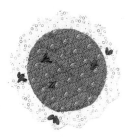

Selina grabbed the fly swatter down from the wall. She swung it back and forth so hard that she hit one of the pies. It fell to the floor sending crumbs and molasses in all directions.

"Oh, Grandma!" Selina cried, lifting her hands above her head and dropping the swatter.

Mother appeared with Benjamin in her arms. "What's all this?" she cried.

Just then the back door swung open and Father and Henry walked in.

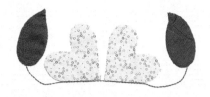

"I smell Shoo-Fly Pies!" Henry exclaimed and picked up the fly swatter. "Maybe I should do the shooing for you, Selina." He scooped up the fallen pie and placed it on the table. Selina saw that he was smiling.

Everyone was amazed at the sudden change in Henry. Father beamed proudly as he announced, "Henry worked with us at the mill today instead of watching. And he did such good work that he has been given a job for as long as he is here."

Henry put the swatter down. He stood straight and tall, looking directly at all of them.

"I have made up my mind. Some day I am going to build houses — here, in Upper Canada. Houses that will never be blown to bits with cannons and gunfire."

Selina ran to Henry and threw her arms around him. "I'll bake your Shoo-Fly Pies if you do, Henry," she said solemnly. "You can have a piece every day."

Henry winked at Grandmother. "I think I should taste one first, Selina, just to be sure."

Father laughed and patted Henry on the back. Before long, even before supper, everyone was eating Selina's Shoo-Fly Pie.

HOW TO MAKE SHOO-FLY PIE

Here are two easy recipes for Shoo-Fly Pie. This dessert was a traditional favorite in many Upper Canada kitchens because it kept well and it was so rich that a little went a long way.

Henry's Favorite

Pastry for one deep-crust, 9 inch pie

Bottom part:
1/2 cup molasses
1 teaspoon soda
1 cup boiling water
pinch of salt

Top part:
1 1/2 cups flour
1 cup brown sugar
3/4 cup butter or lard
1/2 teaspoon cinnamon

Dissolve the soda and salt in the molasses and stir until it foams; add the boiling water. Mix the flour, cinnamon, sugar and butter into crumbs. Pour one-third of the liquid into the unbaked crust; sprinkle one-third of the crumbs over the liquid and continue alternating layers, putting the crumbs on top. Bake in a 375° F oven for about half an hour until the crumbs and crust are golden.

Shoo-Fly Pie With a Wet Bottom

Pastry for one deep-crust, 9 inch pie

Bottom part:
3/4 cup boiling water
1/2 teaspoon soda
1 cup dark molasses

Top part:
1 1/2 cups sifted flour
1 cup brown sugar
3/4 cup shortening
1/4 teaspoon salt

Pour boiling water over soda in a bowl and stir in molasses. Pour into the pie shell. Mix ingredients for crumbs and sprinkle over the molasses mixture. Bake in a 350° F oven for 30 to 40 minutes. Let cool and slather it with whipped cream.

From FOOD THAT REALLY SCHMECKS Mennonite Country Cooking, *by Edna Staebler, McGraw Hill Ryerson, 1968, with kind permission.*